TOWER HAM

KT-178-837

91 000 004 397 25 3

I am not a Loser

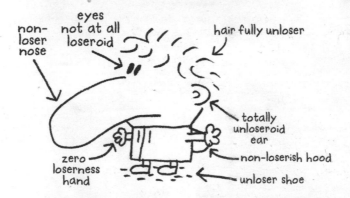

non-loser nose

eyes not at all loseroid

hair fully unloser

totally unloseroid ear

non-loserish hood

zero loserness hand

unloser shoe

Barry Loser

Spellchecked by Jim Smith

Jelly Pie

EGMONT

EGMONT

First published in Great Britain 2012
by Jelly Pie an imprint of Egmont UK Ltd

The Yellow Building, 1 Nicholas Road, London W11 4AN

Text and illustration copyright © Jim Smith 2012
The moral rights of the author-illustrator have been asserted.

ISBN 978 1 4052 6031 2

3 5 7 9 10 8 6 4

barryloser.com
www.egmont.co.uk

A CIP catalogue record for this title is available from the British Library

Printed and bound in Great Britain by the CPI Group

49953/9

All rights reserved. No part of this publication may be reproduced,
stored in a retrieval system, or transmitted, in any form or by any means,
electronic, mechanical, photocopying, recording or otherwise, without the prior
permission of the publisher and copyright owner.

Stay safe online. Any website addresses listed in this book/magazine are correct at the time of
going to print. However, Egmont is not responsible for content hosted by third parties. Please be
aware that online content can be subject to change and websites can contain content that is
unsuitable for children. We advise that all children are supervised when using the internet.

MIX
Paper
FSC FSC® C018306

EGMONT LUCKY COIN

Our story began over a century ago, when seventeen-year-old
Egmont Harald Petersen found a coin in the street.

He was on his way to buy a flyswatter, a small hand-operated
printing machine that he then set up in his tiny apartment.

The coin brought him such good luck that today Egmont has
offices in over 30 countries around the world. And that lucky
coin is still kept at the company's head offices in Denmark.

Praise for my other books

'Will make you laugh out loud, cringe and snigger, all at the same time'
-LoveReading4Kids

'Very funny and cheeky'
-Booktictac, Guardian Online Review

Waterstones Children's Book Prize Shortlistee!

'I LAUGHED SO MUCH, I THOUGHT THAT I WAS GOING TO BURST!'
Finbar, aged 9

'The review of the eight year old boy in our house... "Can I keep it to give to a friend?" Best recommendation you can get' -Observer

'HUGELY ENJOYABLE, SURREAL CHAOS'
-Guardian

I am still not a Loser
WINNER of
The Roald Dahl
FUNNY PRIZE
2013

Library Learning Information

To renew this item call:

0115 929 3388

or visit

www.ideastore.co.uk

TOWER HAMLETS

Created and managed by Tower Hamlets Council

TOWER HAMLETS LIBRARIES	
91000004397253	
Bertrams	01/07/2014
J	£5.99
THISCH	TH14000491

Being a Loser

I've never minded that my name's
Barry Loser because my coolness has
always cancelled it out, but ever since
Darren Darrenofski joined school with
his horrible little crocodile face he's been
completely ruining my life about it.

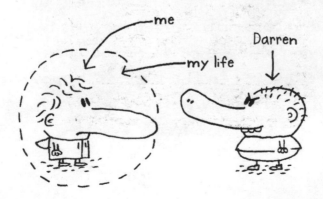

me

my life

Darren

Ringpull

He's always slurping on cans of Fronkle then burping in my ear.

When I complain that the burp is really loud and stinks of Fronkle he does this annoying little dance and sings 'Barry Loser's a Loser' to the tune of 'Happy Birthday to You', which doesn't work because it's got too many syllables.

'At least I don't look like a poo bum crocodile,' I said back, which sounded a bit loserish when it came out of my mouth but it confused him enough so that I could run off before he threw his whole can of Fronkle at me.

Darren had got me worried that my laces were too long though and I spent the whole of Maths measuring shoelace lengths and came to the conclusion that he was right, so when I got home I cut a bit off each one.

Mr Hodgepodge   Tracy Pilchard   Darren Darrenofski

Bunky   Anton Mildew   Stuart Shmendrix

Sharonella   Fay Snoggles   Me

By the way I'm a child genius so I didn't just throw the leftovers away, I came up with an amazing use for them.

I planted them in the back garden like they were worms and watched from my window with my dad's binocs as the little birds tried to eat them.

'Do you want me to grab the end of Darren's nose and stick it in a letter box?' asked my friend Bunky as we walked home from school the next day. Bunky isn't his real name by the way, it's what his mum calls him.

Luckily he hasn't heard my mum calling me 'Snookyflumps', although come to think of it, nothing could be worse than being called Barry Loser.

Dinnnnner, Snookyflumps!

I'm gonna do something about my loserish name before Darren completely ruins my life about it even more.

The Keel Gang

Before Darren I was always one of the cool people at school. Not that I ever say the word 'cool', I say 'keel'. It's something me and Bunky came up with because in our favourite TV show, Future Ratboy, he says it that way.

The Keel Gang is mostly just me and
Bunky hanging out together, watching
Future Ratboy and playing it keel.

I'm **Future Ratboy** and Bunky is his
annoying sidekick, Not Bird, except
Bunky's not a bird and he doesn't say
'NOT' after everything.

One of the other things the Keel Gang does is annoy people down my street by knocking on their doors and running off, then phoning them up asking to speak to Poopoo.

Bunky's favourite person to annoy is Mrs Trumpet Face, who lives in the block of flats at the end of the road with her twin kids and no husband.

In the summer we play wall tennis
against her wall until she yells out of
the window for us to stop, which
is when we run off shouting
'Trumpet Faccccceeeee!', giggling and
blowing off with fear.

Once when it snowed we painted
ourselves blue and pretended we'd
frozen to death outside her flat.
When she saw us she screamed and
started giving Bunky the kiss of life
until we got up and ran off shouting
'Trumpet Faccccceeeee!'

'Ha ha, she kissed you! You're married to Mrs Trumpet Face now!' I said to Bunky after that to annoy him.

I think he secretly liked it though, because for about a year every time I called him Bunky he said, 'Er, my name's Mr Trumpet Face now?' which ended up really annoying me instead.

At lunchtimes the Keel Gang does TV shows in the playground for the other kids. Our favourite is Vending Machine Mum, which is where I play my mum (who's turned into a vending machine) and Bunky plays me.

coin slot

Fronkle is the keelest!

choose flavour

Fronkle comes out here

It's based on how my mum says she feels like a vending machine, always giving me food and ironed clothes and packed lunches without me ever saying thanks.

me next door
watching
Future
Ratboy →

I made the vending machine costume
out of the box the new washing
machine came in after our old one
exploded foam everywhere.

The costume's so brilliant and
amazing that the first time I wore it
Jocelyn Twiggs thought it was real and
followed me around all lunch trying to
get a can of Diet Fronkle out of it.

now playing:
'I Got the Bogie Blues'
by Frankie Teacup
and the Saucers

me

We were in the playground acting
out Vending Machine Mum the other
day and just getting to the bit where
she's making my bed while I'm
completely not helping at all, when
Darren Darrenofski's crocodile face
snuffled into the front row and started
burping Fronkle gas into the scene.

'Poo, what's that smell?' I said, which wasn't in the script.

'Maybe your loser son weed the bed,' said Darren and he threw a ringpull at me, which annoyamazingly went into the coin slot of my costume and everyone laughed.

'Nice shot, Darren!' said Tracy Pilchard, who was in the audience with her stupid gang, which is her, Donnatella and Sharonella. They call themselves 'The Cool Girlz', which is a completely unkeel name in my opinion.

'Yeah,' said Donnatella. 'Nice shotingtons.' They put 'ingtons' on the ends of their words as well, which is also unkeel.

'Er, Darren, we're trying to do our TV show?' I said, all shaking out of anger.

'What's it called? Loseroid City?' he said, and everyone laughed again including Bunky, which I couldn't believe because it was so unfunny.

'No, it's called Darren's Face is All Crocodiley and He's Fat from Too Many Fronkles,' I shouted back.

'No need to be so horrible, Barry Loser,' said Sharonella, and everyone in the crowd said 'yea-eahh!' even though it was Darren who'd started it, not me.

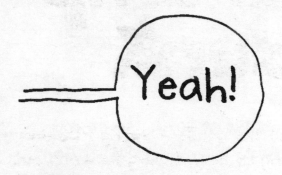

'I've had enough of this!' I shouted and ripped myself out of my costume, storming off with everyone watching and saying how much of a loser I was, Bunky included.

Granny Harump-adunk

Ever since the whole Vending Machine Mum thing I'd been trying to work out how to get back to being one of the keelest people in school.

I'd had a think for about three-quarters of a minute and used my child geniusness to its full extent and come up with a brilliant and amazing plan. There was only one person that could help me with it and that was Granny Harumpadunk.

can't hear

can't see

really slow at walking

Mum's always saying that Granny has lots of 'issues'. At first I thought she was saying 'tissues' and couldn't work out what the big problem was. Then I realised it was 'issues', and even though I don't know what it means I kind of get that Granny is a bit weird.

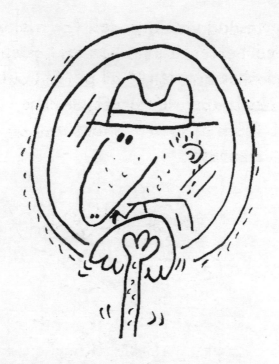

Ever since Grandad died she's been funny. If you go near his old chair she gets all angry. Not that you would go near it, because Invisigrandad is sitting there.

Invisigrandad was my idea for making her feel better. It's his hat and glasses and clothes and stuff all puffed out with newspaper. It's pretty lifelike, apart from it doesn't snore and do massive burps.

For someone who misses someone so much she's still pretty grumpy with him.

'Oh Wilf, will you please stop doing those invisible blowoffs,' she said the other day, knitting a trunk warmer for an elephant she's adopted by post, while me and Bunky were watching **Future Ratboy** on her really old TV.

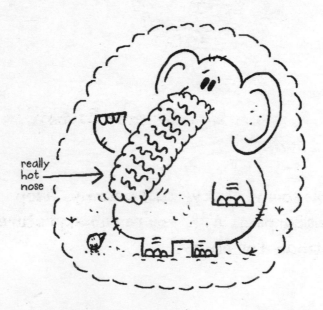

really
hot
nose

'Shhh, you're ruining **Future Ratboy**,'
said Bunky.

'Ooh sorry, Blinky,' said Granny. 'Stop
invisiburping, Wilf, you're ruining **Future
Ratman** for Blinky.'

She's always getting stuff like that
wrong and it took me about twelve
hours to explain my genius plan to her,
but by the end of **Future Ratboy** she'd
got the idea.

'Leave it to me, Barry!' she said and I
put my hand up to high five her and
she grannykissed it.

Barry Fakenose

That's how I came to be walking to school wearing this bright yellow knitted woollen nose.

'You look like an idiot!' said Bunky.

'Er, I look like **Future Ratboy** in the episode where his nose gets run over by a bus?' I said.

'His nose was all flat and keel in that episode. Yours is fat and unkeel.'

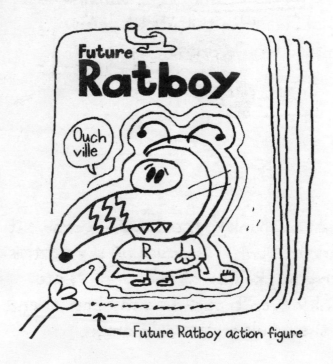

Future Ratboy action figure

'Shut up, Bunky,' I said, but it came out
'Dut up, Dunky,' because of my nostrils
being blocked by all the wool. I hate
Bunky even though he's my best friend
in the whole wide world amen.

The first lesson was Science with
Mr Hodgepodge, who has cross-eyes
and a bent finger so when he points at
someone it's hard to know who he's
talking to.

'What's that monstrosity on your face, Barry Loser?' he shouted, pointing at Anton Mildew and looking at Fay Snoggles.

'It's my **Future Ratboy** nose!' I said, but it came out 'Dit's dy Duture Datdoy dose'.

'Well take it off. You look like an anteater,' he said, so I took it off and put it back on as soon as he looked away, which was immediately.

Because it was so yellow and woolly, as I looked from left to right to read what Mr Hodgepodge was writing on the board all I could see was my nose bobbling around in front of me, which I didn't mind because it blocked out my view of The Cool Girlz.

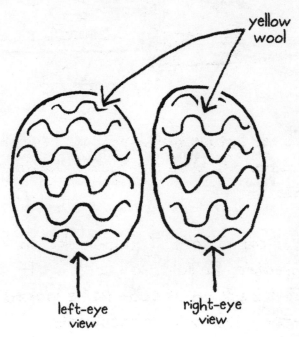

yellow wool

left-eye view

right-eye view

'Ow, your fake nose is hitting my hair,'
said Tracy Pilchard, which was stupid
because it wasn't and hair can't hurt.
'Ow, mine too,' said Donnatella, then
Sharonella said, 'Yeah, mine as
wellingtons,' which I did a chuckle
through my nose about because she'd
said 'wellingtons'.

'It's not funny, Barry Annoyingnose,'
Darren Darrenofski shouted, and
everyone laughed, even Mr Hodgepodge,
then Darren burped in my ear.

'Mmm, dat was dovely, danks Darren,'
I said to confuse him, but I'm not sure
it worked because of my blocked-up
nose and him being thick.

At first break I was really excited
about showing off my nose to
everyone in the playground so
I ran out of Science. The trouble was
that with it bobbling around in front
of me all yellowly I couldn't see
Anton Mildew's lunchbox that he'd left
just lying in the middle of the hall
and I tripped over it and landed right
outside the girls' toilets.

'Serves you right for hurting my hair,'
said Tracy, walking past with her
plastic jewellery all rattling.

'Yeah, Sharonella's got loads of your
woolly bogies in her perm,' Donnatella
said. Sharonella just stood there, and
from where I was lying I could look up
her nostrils and see her ACTUAL bogies.

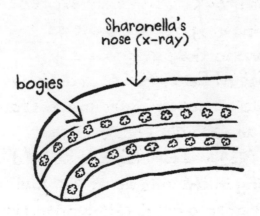

Sharonella's
nose (x-ray)

bogies

'I thought I told you to take that nose off, Barry Anteater,' Mr Hodgepodge said in Art, where we were supposed to be drawing what was right in front of us. My picture was of a really long nose going off into the distance with the wall behind it, which is probably the most boring drawing in the history of the world amen.

At lunch Bunky didn't want to sit opposite me because of my nose taking up so much space, so in front of me there was just an empty chair.

'Having lunch with your invisible friend, Barry Losernose?' said Darren, queuing up for his Fronkle and chips.

'Ha ha, yeah!' chuckled Bunky, leaning over to Anton Mildew. 'Look, Anton! Barry's having lunch with his invisible friend!' he laughed, but Anton didn't join in because he actually HAS got an invisible friend and it gets jealous of other people's.

Time goes slower the longer your nose is and that afternoon was my slowest one ever times ten. Bunky tried to cheer me up on the walk home by ripping my nose off and putting it round his neck, pretending he was Granny Harumpadunk with one of her scarves.

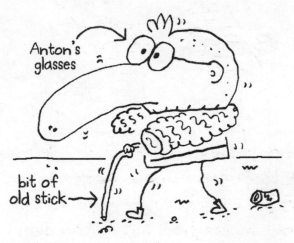

Anton's glasses

bit of old stick →

'Ooh, where did I put my glasses so I can watch Future Ratman,' he said, and I laughed for the first time all day, my head feeling light from the no nose.

Then Darren appeared behind us, all snuffly from running with his Fronkle belly, and started throwing ringpulls at me and singing his 'Loser' song, which ruined my life all over again.

Barry Longlegs

Because it'd been sunny the day before, when I woke up the next morning I had a tan everywhere except where my fake nose had been. I was worried Darren might call me Barry Palenose or something so I decided I'd distract him with one of my genius plans.

Before my grandad got really old, his job was going round at midnight changing the broken light bulbs in lamp posts using stilts instead of a ladder.

Regular　　　Coneboy　　　Old Spikey

Flash　　　The Fist　　　Mr Edges

'Never trust a ladder, Barry,' he'd
shout down at me from his stilts,
wobbling about and waving his arms,
all the light bulbs dropping and
smashing everywhere.

When they sacked him he gave me the
stilts, which is why I was walking to
school with them right now.

'Morning!' I shouted down at Bunky in my Invisigrandad voice, and he looked around, but all he could see were stilt legs and no me.

'Invisigrandad? Is that you?' he said, and I couldn't tell if he was serious.

'Granny Harumpadunk told me you think she's unkeel,' I said, trying to sound scary.

tan gone already

boing

'I-I'm sorry, Invisigrandad, I won't do it again,' Bunky said, then he looked up at me and shouted, 'NOT!'

'Race you to school!' I said and in about three steps I was there, Bunky running as fast as he could but still taking nine hours.

'What's all this crazy business?' said
Mr Hodgepodge when I came into the
classroom.

'It's my new look!' I shouted down at
him. 'Keel times ten or what!'

'Outside now, Loser!' he shouted,
pointing at Donnatella and looking at
Sharonella.

'That's not fair!' cried Donnatella and she burst into tears.

Tracy Pilchard ran over, screeching, 'Emergency group-huggingtons!' and they all cuddled each other until Tracy Pilchard noticed Sharonella's new hairband and they started talking about that instead.

quiver

That was about as good as the
morning got for me, what with
Mr Hodgepodge explaining for the
billionth time to The Cool Girlz about
his cross-eyes and bent finger, then
making me stand outside for the whole
rest of the lesson like I was a tree.

'Mr Hodgepodge, it's raining,' I shouted after nineteen hours, even though it wasn't, but he was too busy telling Stuart Shmendrix to stop flicking his bogies at Jocelyn Twiggs to hear me. Darren, who sits in the back row, had turned his chair round and was staring at me through the glass.

'Mr Hodge-podge, it's wain-ing,' he
mouthed in a loserish way, waving
his arms around like branches, which
got me worried that that was what I
looked like, so for the rest of the
lesson I kept quiet and made a story up
in my head about a tree falling on him.

At lunch I could see down into everybody's lunchboxes because of how tall I was, which was actually really boring.

'Here, ducky!' Bunky was saying, throwing bits of food into my mouth but missing, half of it landing in Sharonella's hair, which was on top of her stupid head.

tremble

'Sharonella's got sandwiches and crisps in her hair, Barry Stupidlegs,' Tracy Pilchard shouted at me from the ground, and I was worried she could see the bogies up MY nostrils.

'Ha ha, Barry Stupidlegs!' laughed Bunky and I stepped on his toe with my stilt then said sorry then whispered 'not'.

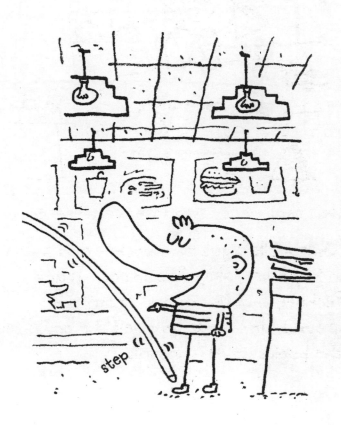

step

It was Games in the afternoon, which was really easy because we were doing running.

'Work those stilts, Loser!' Mr Koops the Sports teacher was shouting through his megaphone, and I felt pretty keel because usually he doesn't even know who I am.

'Watch this, Mr Koops!' Darren said and he made his little legs go as fast as he could but I still beat him easily with one step.

'No Banana, Darrenofski,' shouted Mr Koops, which is one of his favourite catchphrases. I've never seen him with any actual bananas though so it's lucky no one ever runs fast enough to win one.

On the way home with Bunky I was
thinking how my day hadn't been the
worst one of my whole life ever, when
I stopped to cross the road for about
a millisecond and looked down and saw
that someone had stuck a poster to
my legpoles.

Darren was running off cackling, and seeing as I know Darren's dad is a poster putter-upperer because he came into school one Friday afternoon to talk all about it, I suppose it was him that must have put it there.

'Maybe you should just go back to being rubbish old Barry Loser again,' said Bunky.

'Thanks, Bunky, that makes me feel so much better,' I said in the voice **Future Ratboy** uses when he hates Not Bird, and I stormed off home with my stilts making it really hard to storm.

Play it keel with Fronkle!

Barry Massive Robot Barry

'How was your day, Snookyflumps?'
my mum said when I got home.

'Rubbish,' I said, handing her my stilts, and she gave me a massive hug, which I squirmed out of but secretly quite liked. 'I'm gonna do my homework,' I said and went upstairs.

Once I was in my room I threw my bag on the floor and went over to the Vending Machine Mum costume.

There was a **Future Ratboy** episode once where this massive robot came to town and everyone thought he was their new ruler. All I had to do was add a few robotty things to my outfit and I'd have everybody worshipping me too.

At seven o'clock, when me and Bunky usually phone Mrs Trumpet Face to ask if Poopoo is there, the phone rang.

'Barrrrrrrr-ryyy, it's Bunnnnnn-kyyy!' my mum shouted up the stairs.

'Tell him he's a poo bum,' I shouted down the stairs and carried on making my costume until it was time for bed, when I shut my eyes and tried to dream about being a giant robot.

Annoyingly, my dream was about
Darren and his dad putting posters up
all over town saying how much of a
loser I was. So it was good when I
arrived at school the next day in my
Barry Massive Robot Barry
costume and everyone thought an
enormous robot had come to kill them.

KILL ALL
LOSEROIDS

'I think it's eaten Barry!' Bunky was
shouting, because I hadn't walked to
school with him because of our row.
I threw my rucksack out of the mouth
bit of the costume and did a massive
fake burp and Bunky fell to his knees,
holding the bag up to the sky crying
'Barrrryyyyy noooooooooooo!'

'It's the endingtons!' screamed
Sharonella, pushing Tracy Pilchard and
Donnatella over and running off with
her hands waving.

'EVERYBODY PANIC!' crackled
Mr Hodgepodge's voice over the school
speakers, and I saw him run over to his
car and drive off at full speed, his tie
caught in the door all waggling.

Just as I was beginning to worry that it was maybe getting a bit out of hand, Darren Darrenofski's horrible little crocodile voice shouted over everything.

'Ladies and gentlemen, the robot you are all doing blowoffs about is actually just Barry Loser inside a cardboard box. Stop being such Stuart Shmendrixes and go back to your normal rubbish lives.'

Anton's Lunchbox

It was pretty boring having to be inside
the cardboard box for the rest of the
day, which was my punishment from
Mr Hodgepodge once the police had
found him hiding in his attic and
explained everything.

'You're a naughty Loser,' Darren
burped into one of my airholes, and
the word 'Loser' echoed around the
box about seven-million times until I
realised I was stuck with my name so
I might as well stop trying to be
someone else.

My loser haircut

So when I woke up with my mum shouting 'Breakfast, Snookyflumps!' on Saturday morning I was back to being a Loser again.

Bunky was already sitting on the sofa in our living room when I came downstairs. I'm used to this because he spends more time at my house than at his.

'Ah, Bunky, how keelnessly unkeel to see you,' I said in full **Future Ratboy** mode.

'Morning, Snookyflumps!' he chuckled to himself while watching TV and eating breakfast like he was me. I gave my mum one of my evil stares that I've been practising in the mirror for Darren Darrenofski, and stormed out of the house with Bunky behind me.

'I told her not to call me that
any more,' I said on the way to the
hairdressers.

'Call who what?' Bunky said, looking
at me like he didn't know what I was
talking about, which didn't surprise
me because he hardly ever remembers
anything for more than two
milliseconds.

It was my first ever trip to the hairdressers. My mum usually cuts my hair but last time she tried we had a row about how she wasn't doing it right, so she'd booked me, Bunky and Granny Harumpadunk into Harry's on the high street with one of her three-for-the-price-of-two coupons.

On the way to pick up Granny we
walked past Mrs Trumpet Face's flat.
She was shouting at her kids about
something and Bunky pressed his nose
against the window until she saw him
and screamed and we ran off giggling
and blowing off.

'Do we HAVE to go with Granny Harumpaloser? She's so boring,' Bunky said.

'Shhh!' I whispered because I didn't want Granny to hear, even though we were about eight streets away and she's completely deaf.

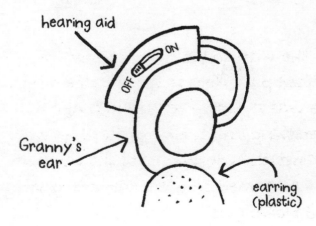

hearing aid

ON

OFF

Granny's ear

earring (plastic)

Granny lives in the most boring road in the whole wide world amen. I've never seen anyone down it, apart from this old grandad who stands outside number Twenty Seven all day feeding the birds mouldy bread.

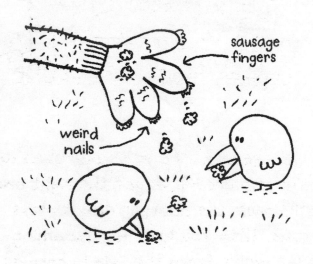

sausage fingers

weird nails

Her house looks like everyone else's and
I'm never sure if I've got the right one
until I press the doorbell and it plays
a tune. Then you hear her humming
as she walks from the living room at
about one mile an hour.

'Helllloooo the Cool Boyz!' said Granny
through the letterbox.

'Hi Granny, how's your keelness level?'
I said, holding up my hand for her to
give me a high five.

'Ooh, not so bad. Now, I've just got to
switch everything off and get my bits,'
she said, then started walking all the
way back to the living room.

'Unkeelness factor nine,' said Bunky
into his watch, which is what **Future
Ratboy** does when he wants to be
beamed out of somewhere.

We played all the songs on Granny's
doorbell while we were waiting,
until the old grandad at Twenty Seven
shouted for us to shut up.

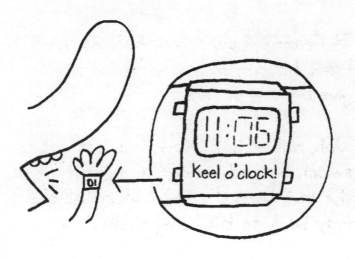

Keel o'clock!

The walk to the hairdressers took ages
as well because we bumped into
Granny's friend Ethel on the way and
they had to have a three hour
natter about the state of the
pavements on the high street.

Some other granny called Doreen had tripped over one last week and her false teeth had fallen down the drain. 'She fished them out with her stick and popped them back in on the spot,' said Ethel, whose feet were too fat for her sandals.

'That's our Doreen,' said Granny, and I imagined Doreen walking down to the shops with bits of old leaves hanging out of her teeth.

We were late by the time we got to Harry's and before I could say, 'Don't cut my ear lobes off,' we were in our chairs.

Bunky and Harry started chatting straight away, even though it was MY hair Harry was cutting, and Granny had stuck her head in a perming machine so I felt a bit loserish, sitting there with no one to talk to.

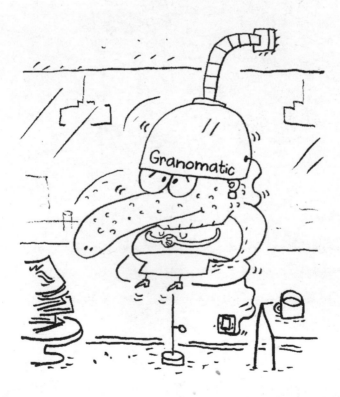

'Have you noticed how our names
rhyme?' I said to Harry, trying to
make him like me, but he just did a
fake laugh and carried on talking to
Bunky.

'Do you remember when we completely ruined Mrs Trumpet Face's day!' I said to Bunky, trying to stop him talking to Harry, but he just looked at me like I was a loser and carried on talking to Harry.

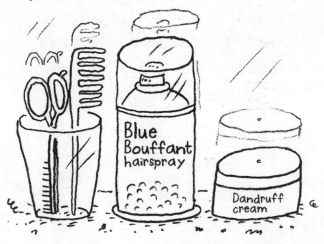

I gave up trying after that and stared at myself in the mirror with my back-to-front superhero cape that they'd put round my neck, imagining I was **Future Ratboy**.

There's a bit in every **Future Ratboy** episode when he takes his mask off and shows his hair to a baddy. He always says 'Operation Reveal the Keel' before he does it and the baddies are so impressed by how shiny and bouncy his hair is that they forget what they're doing and he lassoes them with his tail.

Future Ratboy shampoo advert

When I woke up, not that I'd been asleep, I realised Harry had turned me sideways to do the bits around my ears and I was facing out of the shop like I was a can of hairspray for sale in the window or something.

What was worse was that
Darren Darrenofski was looking at
me from the other side of the glass.

'Nice haircut, Barry Loserhaircut!' he
shouted, his spit splattering the window.
Then he started doing this thing with
his hands, cupping the air behind the
back of his head.

'What are you talking about, Crocodile Face?' I mouthed to him, doing my evil stare, but he probably only saw half of it because Harry was turning me round to face the mirror again.

'Operation Reveal the Keel!' I said as I twizzled round.

TA-DA!

That was when I saw what Darren was talking about. In front of me sat me, except with a massively sticking-out-at-the-back-of-my-head haircut.

'Your head's sticking out miles at the back!' said Bunky, and Harry chuckled, agreeing.

I've always had a big head due to my massive brain, but combined with the way Harry had been cutting my hair while completely ignoring me and chatting to Bunky it now looked ginormingtons.

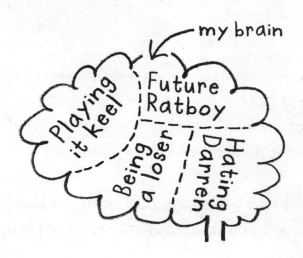

my brain

Playing it keel

Future Ratboy

Being a loser

Hating Darren

'It's not that bad,' said Bunky on the way home, the back of his head not sticking out at all.

'It's not great though, is it, Blinky,' said Granny, whose hair was all frizzy and bright blue now by the way.

The wall-paper show

As if my weekend couldn't get any more loserish and boring, after lunch my mum came into the living room and said, 'We're going to the wallpaper show,' which I knew about because Darren's stupid dad had wallpapered half the town with adverts for it.

So it was my mum and dad, Bunky because he thinks he's one of the family like I've already said, Granny with her blue frizzy hair and me with my massively sticking-out head all walking around this stupid exhibition, when we bumped into Mr Hodgepodge.

Mogden Museum

A History of Wallpaper 1700 - Today

'Bunky and Barry!' he said, pointing
and looking at the wrong one of us
for each name. 'And this must be your
sister!' He was looking at my mum
and pointing at my dad but I realised
straight away he was talking about
Granny.

'Granny, meet Mr Hodgepodge,' I said.
'He's the one who called me an
anteater and laughed when Darren said
I was Barry Annoyingnose, then made
me stand outside like I was a tree.'

'Very pleased to meet you,
Mr Hedgehog,' said Granny and she put
her hand up for him to high five it.

Suddenly I sensed something annoying to my left. I looked out of the window and saw Darren Darrenofski standing there again with his can of Fronkle.

'What is it with you standing behind windows I'm on the other side of?' I mouthed, which is probably the world record for longest-ever mouthed sentence.

'Is that your mum and dad?' he
spitmouthed back, because he hasn't
been at school long enough to spot
Mr H gepodge from behind, which
isn't very hard due to his fat bum.

'No!' I screamed like a girl, not wanting
Darren to think I had really old
parents.

'What are you, Barry Highvoice now?' said Bunky in his rubbish **Future Ratboy** voice, and Mr Hodgepodge and Granny chuckled.

I don't like it when people laugh at me so I said, 'Bunky reckons you've got a fat bum,' to Mr Hodgepodge, whose eyebrows went up about three and a half centimetres. He quickly said goodbye and wobbled away with his exhibition booklet covering his bum.

'What a hunk!' said Granny, looking at Mr Hodgepodge through her glasses, which I think must make everything blurry.

I looked out of the window and saw Darren walking off down the road, his stupid crocodile head working out how to ruin my life because he thinks I've got a granny-and-grandadish mum and dad, even though I don't.

Fronkle-
spit
hairgel

I spent the whole of Sunday trying to flatten down the back of my hair by just lying in bed doing nothing at all, but by Monday morning it was sticking out more than ever.

homework noise to fool Mum

I was nervous as I entered the
classroom, mostly because of my stupid
haircut but also because of the whole
grandparent-parents thing.

Barryitis Loseritum

I could just imagine Darren Darrenofski telling the whole class about how he'd seen me with my really old mum and dad and that my hair was sticking out miles at the back. They were probably all waiting for me to come through the door so they could start laughing.

I needn't have worried, though. Luckily Stuart Shmendrix's little brother had thrown a boiling hot fish finger at his forehead on Saturday afternoon and it'd sizzled into his skin and now he had orange breadcrumbs where his eyebrows used to be.

looking for eyebrow cream

Darren was too busy singing about Stuart's eyebrows to the 'Happy Birthday' tune to notice me coming in with my family-size bottle of Fronkle.

I don't usually drink much Fronkle because my mum says it makes your teeth go short like Granny's, but I needed it to get my spit gloopy so I could gel my sticking-out back-of-hair down.

lid hassle

Cherry Fronkle

Now even more cherrykeelness!

That's what I was doing, licking my
palm with gloopy Fronkle-spit and
spreading it on to my hair, when
Darren faded out his song about
Stuart's fish-finger eyebrows and
looked round the sports hall for
someone else's life to ruin.

It's Games on Mondays at that time so that was why we were in the sports hall. I was in my usual spot at the side with Bunky, trying not to get hit by the ball Mr Koops was throwing at us.

groan

'Dodge the Koopball' is Mr Koops's favourite game for when he can't be bothered to do any teaching. It's just all of us in the hall running for our lives while he throws a ball at us.

124

'Watch out for Barry Loserhaircut, Mr Koops. His mum and dad are about ninety-seven each so he's probably not as strong as the rest of us,' shouted Darren. His wobbly little Fronkle belly made it look like he had the Koopball under his T-shirt.

'That was my granny and Mr Hodgepodge, Crocoloser,' I said, louder than I meant, and my girly screamvoice echoed all round the hall.

'Ha ha! Barry Loser's grandad is
Mr Hodgepodge!' Darren farted out
of his mouth, and everybody stopped
running for their lives and cracked up,
including Mr Koops who doesn't take
teaching seriously enough if you ask
me, especially right now at this exact
moment in the history of the
universe amen.

'We'll see whose grandad is
Mr Hodgepodge outside the gates
after school,' I heard myself
saying, even though I wasn't moving
my mouth. Then I realised it was Bunky
speaking, but by then it was too late
and I had a fight on my hands.

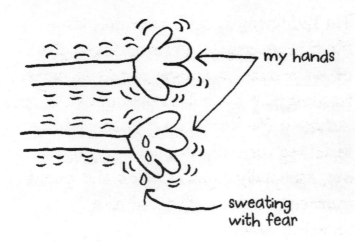

my hands

sweating
with fear

Mr Loser pants

By lunch everyone in the whole school had heard about the fight, mostly because Art comes after Games and Darren had done a really rubbish poster saying 'Darren Darrenofski V Barry Loserhaircut' with the date and time on it, then photocopied it a million times and put them up everywhere, including sticking one to my bum for about two seconds.

'Darren's gonna eat you for breakfast,
Barry Loserhaircuttingtons,' said
Tracy Pilchard, with Donnatella and
Sharonella behind her.

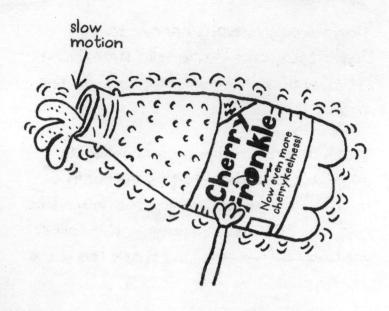

slow
motion

'Don't you mean for tea?' I said back,
after a massive gap where I was
trying to think of something clever to
say. I took a sip from my Fronkle but
my neck was shaking from being
worried about the fight, so the bottle
bashed against my face and Fronkle
sloshed down my jumper.

'Don't wee yourself, Barry,' said Donnatella, and Sharonella snarfled a little laugh, putting an 'ingtons' on the end of it.

Because I'd been drinking Fronkle all day I actually did need to go for a massive wee, but I'd been too scared to risk it in case Darren was in the toilets waiting to flush me down the loo like a smelly poo.

So I was jiggling my legs around and doing little dances and singing the theme tune to **Future Ratboy** to stop myself weeing my pants when the end of school bell rang. I usually like that noise, but this time it sounded like the worst alarm clock ever in the history of the world amen.

I was like one of those massive sharks you see on TV that have loads of little fish swimming around them as I jiggled towards the gates with Bunky and Stuart Shmendrix and all the other hangers on giggling and talking about the fight and how Darren was going to beat me easily.

'I think the pressure's really getting to him,' said Bunky into the banana that Anton Mildew was holding up to his mouth like a microphone.

'This is Anton Mildew reporting live from the big fight,' said Anton to his invisible cameraman, then he peeled the banana and ate it in about a second flat and threw the skin on the floor in front of Fay Snoggles, who didn't slip on it.

Darren was facing the other way when I got to the gates.

'Ah, Mr Loserpants, so nice of you to join me,' he said, twizzling round with a Fronkle in his hand and trying to sound like a film baddy.

'Oh yeah, I REALLY want to join you by the bit of wall you're standing next to. Does it remind you of the zoo your crocodile mum lives in?' I said. I didn't really know what I was talking about.

Everybody was chanting 'fight!' by now, Bunky included, who was jumping around doing boxing moves.

'Don't talk about my mum,' said Darren. He'd walked right up to me and I could smell the Fronkle on his breath.

'Mmm, your breath is so Fronkley,' I said in my **Future Ratboy** sarcastic voice that he uses when he's making Not Bird look stupid.

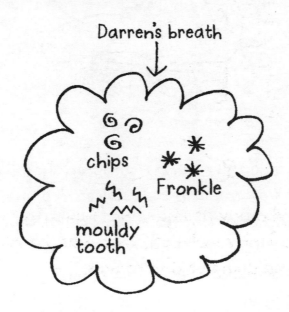

Darren's breath

chips

Fronkle

mouldy tooth

'Yuck, Barry likes smelling Darren's breath!' Stuart Shmendrix shouted from the crowd, with his orange fish-finger eyebrows waggling around.

fight! fight!

I watched my hands come up shakily in front of me and started to feel quite excited about being in an actual fight, when suddenly I heard Donnatella's horrible voice screaming behind us.

'Something terrible's happened,' she cried. Looking back at the school doors I saw Mr Hodgepodge with Sharonella, who was crying, and everyone that'd just been chanting 'fight!' began running towards them, Darren included.

'You're lucky, Barry Loserface,' he burped over his shoulder, which I suppose I sort of was apart from I'd just weed myself.

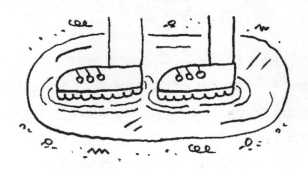

Sort of genius plan

I had to waddle home at full waddle speed with my trousers all wet from Fronkle wee before anyone noticed after that so it was only when Bunky came round later that I found out what had happened.

'There's gonna be a talent contest!' he screamed through the letter box before I'd even opened the door.

'Is that the terrible news?' I said,
looking through the spyhole to see if
he knew I'd weed myself.

'No, that was Sharonella. She slipped on
a banana skin running to sign up for
it,' said Bunky. 'First prize is a Future
Ratboy costume! We could win it
easily with Vending Machine Mum!'
I still hadn't opened the door yet by
the way.

Once he got inside he started dancing around like me when I'd needed my wee, and telling everyone in sight about the talent contest, the only people in sight being me and my mum who he called 'Mum' by accident, embarrassingly for him.

'Aren't you excited?' he said, his voice bouncing up and down.

'Yeah, it's keel, I'm just annoyed I didn't get to punch Crocodile Face in the nose,' I said, but I was lying. I was glad the fight had stopped, I just felt like a massive loser for weeing myself.

'You should get him with one of your genius plans,' said Bunky, and immediately my child geniusness came up with the most brilliant and amazing plan ever in the history of the world amen.

The plan was that I'd tell Darren there
was a new flavour of Fronkle
coming out, which there wasn't at all,
and he'd get all excited and look like a
loser when I told him it was a lie.

'What do you reckon?' I asked later
round Granny's house, after I'd told
her and Bunky the plan.

'It's not your best,' said Bunky. He was busy watching **Future Ratboy** on Granny's old TV.

'Blinky's right, Barry. Can't you come up with something better than that?' said Granny. But I just ignored them both and watched **Future Ratboy**, which was brilliant as usual, like me.

Operation Reveal the Keel

The next day at school the whole playground was full of everyone practising their rubbish acts for the talent contest, which was a complete waste of time for them all because it was obvious me and Bunky would win with Vending Machine Mum.

Bunky and me found Darren round the back of the sports hall wearing an eye mask and throwing ringpulls at Stuart Shmendrix, who he'd tied on to a dustbin lid that was nailed to a traffic cone and was being spun round by Anton Mildew.

'What's all this unkeelness about?' I said in my **Future Ratboy** voice, but also with a bit of action-hero edge because of the nonfight the day before.

'It's mine and Darren's act for the talent contest!' said Stuart, his voice going round and round.

'I'm just helping them out. My act's about the history of sandwiches,' said Anton.

'Whatev. Just thought you'd wanna know there's a new Fronkle flavour coming out,' I said. 'My dad works there, he told me.'

My dad doesn't work there, by the way, he works in an office doing something I can't remember.

Darren stopped throwing ringpulls at Stuart and took his mask off. 'What flavour?' he said, trying not to sound too excited.

'Banana,' I said, because I'd just seen Sharonella limping past with her banana accident leg in plaster.

'Yeaaa-hhh, ba-naaa-naaa,' said Bunky, waving his arms and legs around to make it sound better.

'What's going on here?' shouted
Mr Koops's voice all of a sudden.
'Shmendrix, get down off that
contraption.'

Darren untied Stuart and he staggered
into the playground like a lamp post
that's been bent in half.

'Terribly sorry, Mr Koops, we were just practising our act for the talent contest,' said Darren in his best voice.

'No banana, Darrenofski. Give me a lap of the playground,' Mr Koops shouted, and Darren jogged off, winking at me and doing a little dance like he needed a Banana Fronkle wee.

Darren Darre-nicey

Suddenly everywhere I went Darren was there not calling me a loser or throwing ringpulls at me.

Like on my walk to school, he suddenly appeared behind me all snuffly and panting because he'd had to run to catch up.

'Any news on the Banana Fronkle?' he said, drinking his morning Fronkle.

I could just imagine his crocodile nose drooping to the floor with disappointment when I told him there was no such thing.

Disappointed Darren flavour Fronkle

'I've written an email to Fronkle head office asking if they could send me a sample but I haven't heard back yet,' he burped, being careful that it didn't go in my ear.

I almost felt sorry for him, except I could remember what a horrible little fatbelly he'd been to me all those times. This was the person that'd told everyone I had grandparent-parents and ruined my Vending Machine Mum show with his poo breath and sung 'Barry Loser's a Loser' to the tune of 'Happy Birthday'.

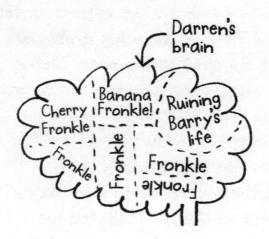

Darren's brain

Banana Fronkle!

Cherry Fronkle

Ruining Barry's life

Fronkle

Fronkle

Fronkle

Fronkle

We chatted about the talent contest
for the rest of the walk and how
Stuart Shmendrix had been feeling
really dizzy recently, for some reason.
Darren thought it might be his
fish-finger eyebrows making
his eyes not know which way
round they were, and I said maybe
he'd end up like Mr Hodgepodge,
all cross-eyed, and we laughed.

'How's your Vending Machine Mum practicing coming along?' said Darren at lunch the next day. He'd squidged himself next to me, which I didn't mind because Anton Mildew had been eating a sandwich in my ear while talking to his invisible friend opposite, which was really annoying.

'We know it off by heart already,' I said, looking over at Bunky, who was picking his nose and eating it for pudding.

'Yeah, we're just playing it keel,' said Bunky. He smiled and you could see a bit of bogie stuck on his tooth.

'You two are so great in it, you'll definitely win,' said Darren. 'Have you heard anything else about Banana Fronkle?'

'Put it this way,' I said, 'don't eat too many bananas the day of the talent contest'.

'What do you mean?' asked Darren, looking confused.

'Well, you wouldn't want to ruin your appetite.'

'For what?'

'Yeah, what for?' Bunky joined in.

'Banana Fronkle,' I said.

'Oh, I get you,' said Darren, and he did a wink, but I don't think he did get me, especially as there's no such thing as Banana Fronkle.

The talent contest

Instead of practising Vending Machine Mum, me and Bunky had our best week of annoying Mrs Trumpet Face ever.

On Tuesday we spotted her in the supermarket on our way home from school and hid in the aisle behind the washing powder she was looking at.

When she picked up a box Bunky's face
was behind it and she jumped and
dropped it and the powder went all
over her kids.

'Trumpet Faccccceeeee!' we screamed as we ran out laughing, everybody in the whole supermarket thinking how keel we were.

Then on Thursday night we stood outside her window for three hours until we realised she was out. Just as we were leaving she arrived home in her car, which we walked next to singing 'Trumpet Face is a Loser' to the **Future Ratboy** tune as she parked it.

It was exciting going to school for the talent contest the next evening what with all the parents there, and I felt keel standing around backstage with Bunky, waiting to go on like we were famous.

'Good luck, Snookyflumps!' my mum said, giving me a hug, which I squirmed out of and walked away from as fast as possible before someone heard.

Mr Hodgepodge, who'd organised the whole thing, was rushing around with a clipboard with nothing on it and telling everybody it was going to be all right, even though he looked more nervous than anyone.

'Do not panic, people,' he was saying as Granny popped her head round the curtain to wish us luck.

'Mrs Harumpadunk!' he said, and his eyebrows went about seven and a half centimetres further up his forehead than normal.

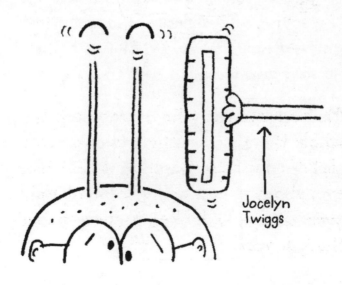

Jocelyn Twiggs

'Ooh, Mr Hedgehog, I do like a man in control of a situation,' said Granny. She stroked her blue frizzy hair but her hand got stuck in it because it's so wiry.

'Some of us are just born leaders, Mrs Harumpadunk,' said Mr Hodgepodge, leaning on the lever that controlled the trapdoor. There was a clunk and then the sound of a scream disappearing down a hole. 'Anyway, things to do!' he said and wobbled off towards the stage.

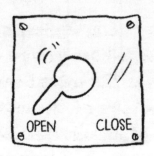

First on were Anton Mildew and his invisible friend, whose lecture about sandwiches was the most boring thing ever in the history of the universe amen and that includes the wallpaper exhibition my mum made us go to.

I was standing there thinking how
amazing I was, while also being
really nervous about my act, when
Mr Hodgepodge came up to me all
sweating and eyes rolling.

'Barry, some idiot's set the trapdoor
off and Fay Snoggles fell through it.
You're good at things like this. Any
ideas?'

'You could climb down and get her?'
I said in my **Future Ratboy** obvious-
answer-to-stupid-question voice.

'Brilliant! Off you go,' he said and he
pushed me on to the stage before I
could say, 'Don't cut my ear lobes off,'
which wouldn't have made much sense
but who cares.

Still the talent contest

The trapdoor was right in the middle of the stage and I didn't want my mum to see me and shout out 'Woooohooooo, Snookyflumps!' so I hid behind Anton's sandwich explainer board and tiptoed towards it as the crowd listened to his talk.

'That board just moved!' shouted someone in the audience who sounded like Darren's dad, but I couldn't be sure because I'd already slipped through the trapdoor and under the floorboards.

The crowd's applause for Anton's lecture was muffled and smelled of damp and was pitch black, although some of that was probably down to me being where I was.

'Fay? Can you hear me?' I whisper-shouted. 'It's Barry! I've come to rescue you but only because Mr Hodgepodge made me.'

Above me someone fat was clomping on to the stage.

'Ladies and gentlemen, please put your hands together for The Cool Girlz!' Mr Hodgepodge's voice said, and I looked through a tiny hole and saw right up one of Sharonella's nostrils, which was full of bogies as per usual.

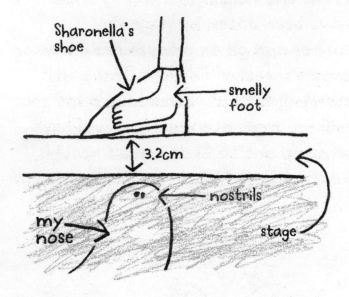

Sharonella's shoe

smelly foot

3.2cm

nostrils

my nose

stage

'I'm on in two acts' time!' I whisper-
shouted into the darkness, but nobody
answered. 'Fay! Fay! Fay! Fay! Fay!
Fay! Fay! Fay! Fay! Fay!' I said in every
direction, turning around like Stuart
Shmendrix on his dustbin lid.

In the end I decided that Fay must have been eaten by a giant sabre-toothed woodlouse and I walked over to where I thought Bunky was standing so that he could help me get out before it ate me too. I could tell when I'd got to him because I could hear his stupid laugh vibrating through the floorboards.

I knocked where I thought his foot was.

'Invisigrandad? Is that you?' he said.

'Yes,' I replied, because I was running out of time. 'Barry's in big trouble. He's stuck under the stage and needs you to get him out.'

'Ha ha, nice one, Invisigrandad, you almost got me there even though you didn't at all,' said Bunky. 'Fay, come and listen to this!'

'What?' said Fay's voice, as if it was right next to me.

'Fay, meet Invisigrandad,' said Bunky, and I looked up through a hole in the floorboards and there was Fay Snoggles, next to Bunky and not at all underneath the stage like me.

'Hello,' she said, but I ignored her and stormed off into the darkness really scared because I was all on my own with the sabre-toothed woodlouse.

Even stiller the talent contest

The Cool Girlz's rubbish dance act was coming to an end above my head.

'Behold as Sharonella flies through the air like a fly, does three somersaults then lands on Donnatella's shoulders!' said Tracy Pilchard's voice. There was a big gasp from the audience, then a massive thud.

ol Girlz

'Helpingtons,' cried Donnatella, who sounded like she was underneath something heavy, like a Sharonella.

'I'm sorry, Donnatella,' Sharonella cried as she was carried off, and Tracy Pilchard did a bow, which I could tell because all her plastic jewellery was rattling.

The Coo

My act was in one act's time now and I was beginning to panic a bit.

'Somebody get me out of heerrreee!' I screamed, but the crowd was clapping too loud to hear. Above me, crocodile face Darren Darrenofski was trotting on to the stage with Stuart Shmendrix.

'Ladies and gentlelosers, I will now throw these sharpened ringpulls at Mr Shmendrix's body as it rotates on the dustbin lid of death!' Darren said.

Mr Hodgepodge's eyebrows must have disappeared over the top of his head or something because now I could hear Granny chuckle to herself somewhere in the front row.

The audience gasped as Darren threw
the ringpulls and I imagined them
shaving past Stuart's upside-down
face and thunking into the metal
behind him.

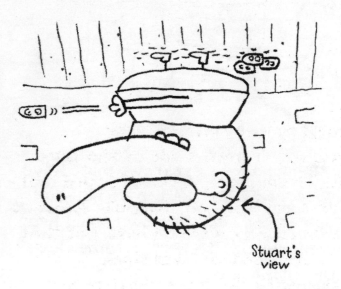

Stuart's
view

I could picture Anton Mildew
watching from the side of the stage
with his sandwich explainer board and
I felt sorry for him, especially seeing as
me and Bunky were on next, not that
we were, because I was stuck
underneath the stage about to be
eaten by the woodlouse.

There was only one person that could help me now, and that was Granny Harumpadunk. I made my way over to the front bit of the stage and started looking for a hole to see her through.

There were two perfect ones right near the floor but to see through them I had to get down on my hands and knees so that my lips were touching the ground. They brushed past a bit of hundred-year-old chewing gum which still smelt of mint but also dust and ant poo.

'Is Barry's dad here?' I heard Darren say to Bunky as he came off the stage and I did a chuckle to myself, even though I was still really scared of the woodlouse.

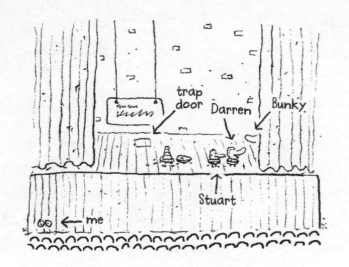

Darren's hand

'Yeah, and he's got a six pack of Banana Fronkle!' said Bunky, and I heard Darren do a little dance and ask for a high five, but by now Bunky must have been beginning to wonder where I was, because he didn't give one back.

Mr Twiggs   Mrs Snoggles   Mrs Sharonella

Mr Pilchard   Mr Donnatella   Mrs Darrenofski

I poked my eyes through the little holes and looked around like one of those paintings in a haunted house.
Annoyingly all I could see of the crowd were their feet.

My granny wears really boring normal shoes and there were about a million of them. I was just about to give up when I spotted Ethel's fat sandal toes pointing right at me. I've never been so happy to see her disgusting smelly feet in my life.

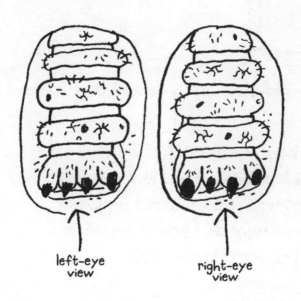

left-eye
view

right-eye
view

'Granny!' I shouted, putting my mouth up to the holes. As I guessed, she was sitting next to Ethel.

'Barry? Is that you?' she said, putting her nostrils right up to my eyes. I looked up them and saw her dried up old granny bogies and sighed a sigh of relief.

Still even stiller the talent contest

'Granny, I'm stuck down here and my act's on next!' I said. 'The trapdoor lever is backstage. Get to it as fast as you can!'

'OK, love, I'll just get my bits,' she said, and I could see her boring shoes shuffle back to her chair at about one mile an hour.

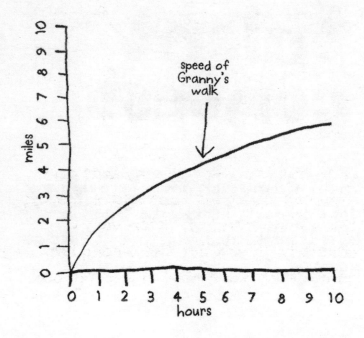

I ran over to where Bunky was and knocked under his foot again. 'Bunky, this is Invisigrandad. Listen very carefully. If you get this wrong I'm gonna stick your nose in a letter box.'

Above me I heard Mr Hodgepodge's loserish voice. 'Ladies and gentlemen, the next act has been called off because Barry Loser has mysteriously disappeared.'

I was standing on the little platform underneath the trapdoor just about to use my girly screamvoice when there was a scraping on the floorboards.

'What's all this crazy business, Bunky? You can't do the act on your own,' mufflewhispered Mr Hodgepodge.

'Orders of Invisigrandad,' said Bunky, and the scraping stopped right above my head.

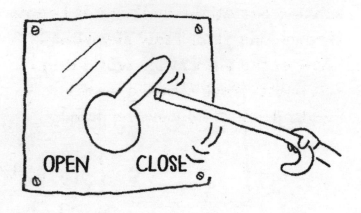

'Operation Reveal the Coolness!'
Granny shouted, and suddenly the
trapdoor flipped open and my Vending
Machine Mum costume dropped on to
my head and the platform started
to rise.

Looking out at the audience as I came through the floor I saw everyone I knew in the whole wide world and I felt pretty keel, chewing on my hundred-year-old chewing gum.

Vending Machine Mum

'I can't remember my lines,' Bunky whisperlaughed next to me, and my heartbeat started echoing inside the cardboard box.

I stared out at the audience and saw everyone's eyes looking back at me, apart from Mr Hodgepodge's, which were pointing at the fire extinguisher and a light switch.

left-eye view

right-eye view

'It was an ordinary night at number Twenty Two Smelly Poo Bum Road . . .' I said in my clearest voice, which is the first line of Vending Machine Mum and everyone in the audience laughed and I smiled with relief inside my costume.

Luckily the school is near an airport and there was a massive plane flying over for the whole of Bunky's main talking bit, so the audience couldn't tell that he was singing the **Future Ratboy** theme tune instead of doing his lines.

I even saw my mum wipe her eye with Dad's hanky at the bit where the me character is just lying there watching **Future Ratboy**, while the mum hoovers around him at the same time as cooking him chicken kiev with chips and peas and doing the ironing.

'That's my Snookyflumps!' she cried as
we walked offstage to applause, me
slapping Bunky on the back and saying
'Good work, Snooky,' to make people
think it was HIS nickname and not
mine.

After us there were about eight
million more acts, which were all
rubbish and three-quarters. Then
suddenly, out of nowhere,
Mr Hodgepodge was introducing a
brother and sister whose names rang
a bell inside my head, which was still
inside the vending machine costume
by the way.

'Ladies and gentlemen, the
Trumpet Face twins!' he shouted, and
Mrs Trumpet Face's twin kids walked
on stage. I looked over at Bunky and
he smiled proudly. I think he thinks he's
actually their dad just because I said he
was Mr Trumpet Face that time.

'We're the Unkeel Gang!' shouted the boy Trumpet Face twin.

'Yeah,' said the girl Trumpet Face twin, 'and we like knocking on people's doors then running off doing farts cos we're so scared!' Then they ran around the stage doing blowoff noises and looking like the biggest losers ever.

Their play went on for ages and the
audience loved it, laughing and
nudging each other and saying, 'It's so
true to life!'

The end was them on the phone calling some old granny and asking if Poopoo was there and a poo coming on the phone telling them they were losers and them crying.

Bunky whooped and cheered along with everyone else and I stamped on his foot and then apologised, calling him Snookyflumps again.

Being a winner

First prize went to the Trumpet Face twins for their 'hilarious and realistic portrayal of loserness'.

I clapped with my little fingers as they stood there and said how they would share the **Future Ratboy** costume, all the parents whispering about how mature they were and Mrs Trumpet Face coming up and cuddling them and everyone getting all emotional about it.

Darren and Stuart came second, winning a month's supply of Fronkle organised by Fay Snoggles's Dad, who works for Fronkle and who said he'd never heard of a Mr Loser working in his office and that no, Banana Fronkle was not coming out soon.

It was weird looking at Darren, because he was stuck between being the happiest person in the whole wide world amen, due to winning a month's supply of Fronkle, and the most annoyed because of me lying to him.

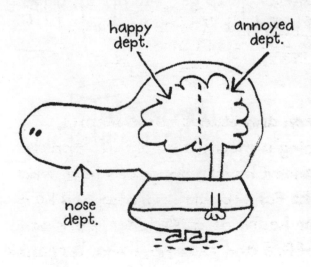

happy
dept.

annoyed
dept.

nose
dept.

I was starting to get my vending machine costume out of there before he came and found me when I heard Mr Hodgepodge announce third place. It went to Barry Loser and Bunky for Vending Machine Mum, which was us and that was our act, so we went up on the stage to get our prizes, giggling and blowing off with keelness.

Being a loser again

After that the local paper did a story about the school talent contest and there was a photo of Darren on the front page having a bath in Fronkle while drinking Fronkle.

The title was 'The Fronkle Kid' and
there was a quote from Darren that
was just a burp that went on for two
pages.

The Trumpet Face twins got so famous at school they had to have a security guard, who looked like an action hero and drove Mrs Trumpet Face around everywhere. I think Bunky was jealous because he still thinks he's Mr Trumpet Face.

What's rubbish is that after the talent contest, Mrs Trumpet Face told my mum about me and Bunky and my mum made us write her a sorry note.

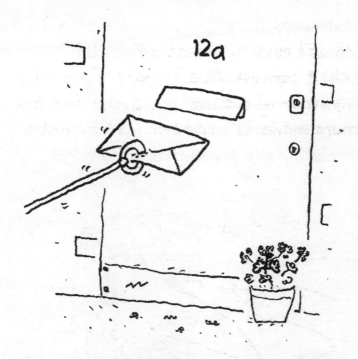

SORRY FOR COMPLETELY RUINING YOUR
LIFE, it said, Mrs Trumpet Face catching
us as we were putting it through her
letter box and inviting us in for biscuits
and Fronkle and a look at the **Future
Ratboy** costume.

'Can I try it on?' I said, hoping she'd forgotten how horrible I was.

'Let me think about that,' she said, but she still hasn't let me so I think that's probably my punishment from her.

What's also rubbish is that third prize
was a roll of grannyish wallpaper
from the wallpaper exhibition, which
my mum and dad made me wallpaper
my bedroom with so now it looks like
Granny's lounge except it hasn't got
Invisigrandad in it.

Not that Granny's lounge has got
Invisigrandad in it either any more,
since she cleared him out because of
Mr Hodgepodge coming over every five
seconds for cups of tea and knitting
lessons.

'Can I be in the Keel Gang, too?' he
asked when me and Bunky went over
there the other day.

'Let me think about that,' I said, and
we high fived but he missed because of
his cross-eyes.

Darren Darrenofski stopped being so horrible after the talent contest. When he found out there was no such thing as Banana Fronkle he ran into the playground crying and a bird did a poo on his head.

That's supposed to be good luck, but I'm not sure it is if the poo has what looked like a bit of my old cut-off shoelace in it.

'Sorry I called you a loser even though you are a Loser,' he said to me a few days later at school in the playground.

'Sorry I lied about Banana Fronkle even though you look like a crocodile,' I said back and we laughed and he burped in my ear.

So I'm OK with being Barry Loser again, which is keel.

What's not so keel is that everyone
heard my mum call me Snookyflumps
at the talent contest last week,
Mr Koops included, who can suddenly
remember who I am for the first time
in my life, unfortunatelyingtons.

'What's going on here, Snookyflumps?'
he shouted through his megaphone the
other day, when me, Bunky and Darren
were carving our names into the big
tree in the corner of the playground.

I'd written 'Barry is the keelest' in massive capitals with three exclamation marks and underlined it.

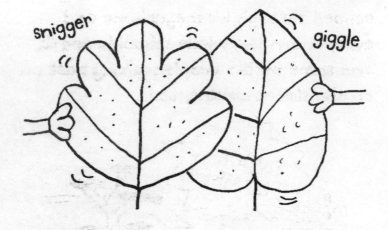

snigger

giggle

'I didn't do it, Mr Koops,' I said in my
nicest voice and Bunky and Darren
started laughing and looking at leaves
like they were really interested in them
so they didn't get in trouble, too.

'No banana,' laughed Mr Koops. 'Give me three laps of the playground, Snookyflumps!' he screeched, and it echoed through his megaphone and everyone in the whole school heard it, and some of the people walking past on the street outside, too.

So now I'm Barry Snookyflumps, which has got to be the most loserish name in the whole wide world amen.

Except for the fact that I secretly quite like it.